# The Cut

## Mark Ravenhill

SAMUELFRENCH.COM
SAMUELFRENCH-LONDON.CO.UK

### FOR PRODUCTION ENQUIRIES

#### UNITED STATES AND CANADA

Info@SamuelFrench.com

1-866-598-8449

#### UNITED KINGDOM AND EUROPE

Plays@SamuelFrench-London.co.uk

020-7255-4302

Each title is subject to availability from Samuel French, depending upon country of performance. Please be aware that *THE CUT* may not be licensed by Samuel French in your territory. Professional and amateur producers should contact the nearest Samuel French office or licensing partner to verify availability.

# CHARACTERS

**Scene One**

**PAUL**

**JOHN**

**GITA**

**Scene Two**

**PAUL**

**SUSAN**

**MINA**

**Scene Three**

**PAUL**

**STEPHEN**

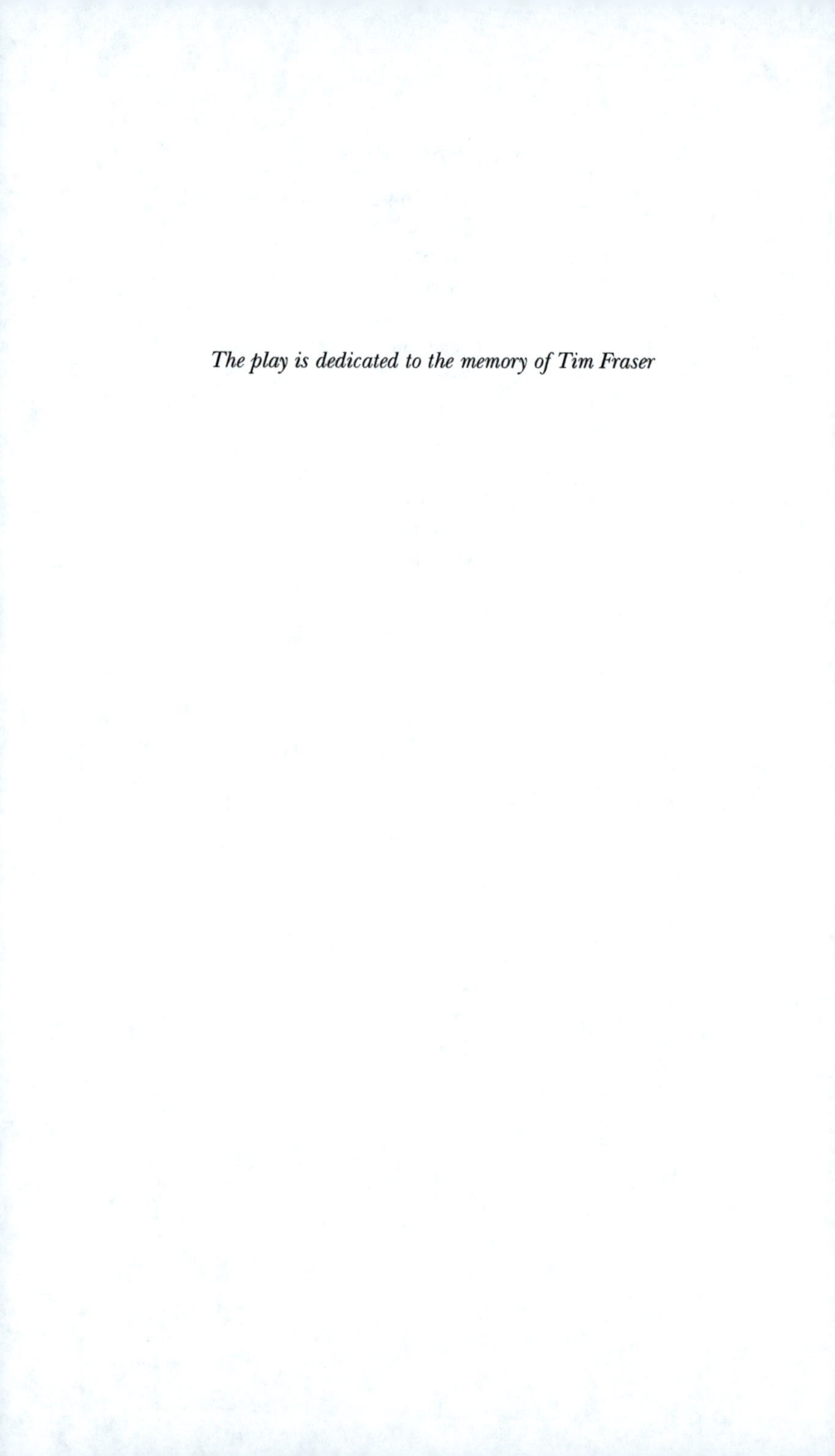

*The play is dedicated to the memory of Tim Fraser*

# Scene One

*(A room. A desk.* **PAUL** *and* **JOHN** *.)*

**PAUL.** Were the searches made?

**JOHN.** I was searched, yes.

**PAUL.** Was there any unnecessary brutality?

**JOHN.** No. No, I wouldn't say it was unnecessary brutality.

**PAUL.** Because I need to record any cases of unnecessary… I'm compiling a dossier. Which many people are eager to read.

**JOHN.** I see.

**PAUL.** The last lot were very slack on unnecessary brutality. Blind eyes were turned. You remember?

**JOHN.** Yes.

**PAUL.** But we intend to be different. We're shining a light on… We're coming down, very hard. You see? On unnecessary…

**JOHN.** Yes.

**PAUL.** But we need the figures, so if you were in any way…

**JOHN.** No, no.

**PAUL.** You have to tell me.

**JOHN.** No.

**PAUL.** Look to you I know I'm – what? – I'm Authority. Power. Strength. The Father.

**JOHN.** Well –

**PAUL.** But honestly you must tell me if there was any unnecessary – for the dossier.

**JOHN.** No.

**PAUL.** You're quite sure?

**JOHN.** Very sure.

PAUL. Well, that's good. Good. Good. No fist?

JOHN. No.

PAUL. No boot?

JOHN. No.

PAUL. Good. Good. Good.

> *(Beat.)*

You were searched?

JOHN. Yes.

PAUL. Thoroughly?

JOHN. Yes.

PAUL. But in such a way as not to…

JOHN. Yes, yes, yes.

PAUL. Good, good, good. You understand why we have to…?

JOHN. Of course.

PAUL. Someone did actually pull a gun on me recently. Little bastard actually got a gun through and pulled it out on me.

JOHN. Shit.

PAUL. And fired.

JOHN. Shit.

PAUL. I actually saw the bullet coming out of the gun, saw it coming towards me and ducked. Just in time.

JOHN. Shit.

PAUL. So as you can imagine I gave those guys out there merry hell. "Security? Security? Call yourself security and you let some fucker through with a gun?" We've had to set a new target for performance. Utterly thorough without any unnecessary brutality. Using that performance indicator, how would you say the operatives did? In your experience?

JOHN. Well…

PAUL. Excellentverygoodgoodaveragepoor?

JOHN. Very good.

**PAUL.** So – some room for improvement. But…getting there. Good.

(**PAUL** *records this in a file.*)

Now. Can I give you any more information?

**JOHN.** No. I don't think so.

**PAUL.** You've read the leaflets?

**JOHN.** I've read everything.

**PAUL.** Well…good, good. Very…impressive.

**JOHN.** I've been preparing for this moment for a long time. Books. The clips. I've thought about this.

**PAUL.** Good.

**JOHN.** I wanted to be ready.

**PAUL.** Excellent.

**JOHN.** I really wanted to be ready for the Cut.

**PAUL.** Yes. Yes. Well, we'll have to see if…

**JOHN.** Where are the instruments?

**PAUL.** They're with –

**JOHN.** Only in the clips they have the instruments all laid out, you know. On the desk. There. Before I…before he…walks into the room they're all laid out and then "Are you ready for the Cut?", "Yes". And – instruments in and –

**PAUL.** Pain.

**JOHN.** Pain and then – done.

**PAUL.** Yes, well – that was the last lot. All very brutal. All very fast. We're…different.

**JOHN.** Yes?

**PAUL.** Oh yes. We're very different. We've made some changes.

**JOHN.** Oh. I see.

**PAUL.** We're a force for change. So…let's consider some other options.

**JOHN.** No.

**PAUL.** We're going to look at –

JOHN. No.

PAUL. No?

JOHN. I want to… I'm here for the Cut. I want the Cut. That's what I'm here for. The Cut.

PAUL. And I'm here to look at the options. And as I'm… as I'm this side of the desk, we're going to look at the options. We're going to look at your choices. Alright?

JOHN. Alright.

PAUL. There's a prison facility. We offer a prison facility to the insane. Are you insane?

JOHN. No.

PAUL. Because if you're insane –

JOHN. I'm not insane.

PAUL. Although prison doesn't come cheap. You pay. Or – poverty pending – we pay. So nobody's keen on the prison facility. Still, if you're actually insane –

JOHN. I'm not.

PAUL. Do you have the paperwork?

JOHN. Here.

*(JOHN hands PAUL a piece of paper.)*

PAUL. Well, this all seems to be…so you're actually sane?

JOHN. Yes.

PAUL. Well that's very impressive. In this day and age. Now, there's the army. Let's think about that.

JOHN. No.

PAUL. Or the university. Maybe we should be sending you to the university.

JOHN. No, no. I don't want –

PAUL. The army and the university. Much more cost-efficient than prison. Let's talk about –

JOHN. No, no, let's not. Let's not mess about.

PAUL. Mess about?

JOHN. Mess about. This, this, this…you're the man who does the Cut, right?

PAUL. I'm in the office of the building where the Cut is –

JOHN. Then do the Cut. Do the Cut on me.

PAUL. This is the office. This is the building. But that doesn't have to define…me. You. We have choices. You and me. We can be…there's the army, the university, the prison. So much choice.

JOHN. No, no.

PAUL. Oh, oh, would you rather be under the last lot?

JOHN. No, no, no.

PAUL. Because if you're telling me you'd rather be under the last lot then that, my son, is a political statement, and if you're making political statements, if you're standing here in a public place – and yes, this is classified as a public place – standing in a public space and making political statements then it's the university for you. I'll send you straight off to the university and they'll soon put a stop to these political statements.

JOHN. No, no, no. I wasn't…there wasn't anything political, just…

PAUL. Yes?

JOHN. Just I've got this far, you know?

PAUL. Of course.

JOHN. Always another office, always another interview, another search, another form to fill. From my village to the town to the city and now…now that I've got this far I thought you'd just…just…

PAUL. Yes?

JOHN. I thought you were a rubber stamp.

PAUL. I am more, I am much much much more than a rubber as you put it stamp.

JOHN. Of course.

PAUL. Would I have all this space, all this facility, all this… fucking impressive… How do I look to you…?

JOHN. Well, yes, impressive.

PAUL. And?

JOHN. And, and…

PAUL. And?

JOHN. Old. As in wise. As in responsible. As in, as in, as in, as in…

PAUL. Authority.

JOHN. Authoritative.

PAUL. As in authoritative authority. Yes. As in burdened with, the burden of…

JOHN. Exactly.

PAUL. Do you think I tell my wife what I do here? (I have a wife.) Do you think my children…? (One's in prison – expensive – one's in university – cheaper.) Do you think I tell my children what I do here? Have you thought about that?

JOHN. Well, maybe you should. Maybe you should. Maybe. Because, listen, the Cut, I think it's… I want the Cut. I think the Cut's a very beautiful…a very old and beautiful…it's a ritual, a custom, something we…

PAUL. I don't think so.

JOHN. To actually leave your body.

PAUL. Have you any idea of the suffering? The pain? The great screams as the instruments go in?

JOHN. Of course.

PAUL. They claw at me. They howl at the sky. It's barbaric.

JOHN. I know all that. All the clips. But I want –

PAUL. And I have to carry all this on. Disgusting. You know we actually – off the record – have a working party looking at, considering ending the whole thing.

JOHN. No.

PAUL. Off the record.

JOHN. Why?

PAUL. Progress. Humanity. Et cetera. Our core values.

JOHN. But that's centuries of…you can't wipe out centuries of…my grandmother, my uncles, so many centuries –

**PAUL.** You can't stand in the way of core values. None of us can.

**JOHN.** Everybody had the Cut.

**PAUL.** And for now of course we're carrying it through.

**JOHN.** Good.

**PAUL.** Just…softening the blow. Talking. We get to know you. You get to know us.

**JOHN.** How does that…?

**PAUL.** For the records.

**JOHN.** Please. I'd like to see the instruments. I don't want to talk.

**PAUL.** I'll be the judge –

**JOHN.** This isn't right. This isn't how it's supposed to be. I'm not supposed to get to know you. You're not supposed to talk to me. You're just supposed to show me the instruments.

**PAUL.** New procedures.

**JOHN.** I haven't heard about –

**PAUL.** There's new procedures all the time. Every day practically. Only this morning I received a directive.

**JOHN.** Where do you keep the instruments?

**PAUL.** New guidelines for talking. Keep things inclusive.

**JOHN.** I don't want to talk.

**PAUL.** If you want to see the directive –

**JOHN.** I'm not going to talk.

**PAUL.** Box files full of the things. Aims. Objectives. Targets. Outcomes. Let me show them. We're very open. It's a root and branch thing.

**JOHN.** No. No. No. Just – Cut me. Come on. Do it. Do it. Show me the instruments. Get the instruments and Cut me.

**PAUL.** Just – like that – cruel, cold, hard, impersonal?

**JOHN.** Yes yes yes.

**PAUL.** That would make me very unhappy. You'd be in great pain –

JOHN. I know that.

PAUL. But also I'd be in great pain. Inside. Enormous pain – physical for you, spiritual for me.

JOHN. Yes. Please. Come on. It's what I want. Fuck's sake – that's what I want.

PAUL. Are you sure you're not insane?

JOHN. You've seen the paperwork –

PAUL. And I suppose we'll have to take their word but still I've never seen anybody so…keen.

JOHN. Yes well…

PAUL. So keen for the Cut. Why are you –?

JOHN. I don't want to talk.

PAUL. Just a little longer.

JOHN. I'd rather we just –

PAUL. Tell me. Tell me and I'll show you the instruments.

JOHN. You've got them?

PAUL. Of course I've got them. Couldn't be in my position unless I had the instruments, could I?

JOHN. Then where…?

PAUL. Ah.

JOHN. In the desk? There's a special drawer in the –?

PAUL. No. Stuffed to the brim with directives. The girl. The girl has the instruments.

JOHN. The girl?

PAUL. Gita. Did you see Gita on your way in?

JOHN. No.

PAUL. Well yes, easily missed, Gita. Can't speak. Can't hear. It's a condition. But we found her a place. Inclusion.

JOHN. Tell her to bring the instruments in.

PAUL. She may be –

JOHN. Tell her to bring the instruments or I won't talk.

> (PAUL *goes to a door, opens it, beckons. Enter* GITA.)

PAUL. You're looking very good today, Gita. We're almost ready. We've almost finished talking and we're almost ready for the instruments. Could you get them ready, Gita? Thank you.

    *(Exit* GITA.*)*

She's very good. Back in a minute. So – tell me. Tell me why you're so different.

JOHN. Am I?

PAUL. Oh yes. Totally different. I've never seen…normally I see fear, anger. Sometimes…sullen, nothing. But you're keen. Because…?

JOHN. Because. Because I want to be free. Free of, of, of me. Of all this. I want it to be Cut away. I want to be Cut away from this body. Yes – and this history and this wanting and this busyness and this schooling and these, these ties. I want to be released.

PAUL. And you think ?/ You really think?

JOHN. Yes yes.

PAUL. You think that's what the Cut –?

JOHN. I know. I know that's what the Cut does.

PAUL. You're very idealistic.

JOHN. I don't think so.

PAUL. Bit of a dreamer.

JOHN. No.

PAUL. Yes, dreamer. Because, look…wouldn't we all? Wouldn't we all like –?

JOHN. We can.

PAUL. We'd all like to be free. Believe me, I want to be free of bodies, of history, of wanting… I'd like that just as much as…

JOHN. Then…free yourself.

PAUL. I can't.

JOHN. You can. Anybody can.

PAUL. No. No. I Cut. You are Cut. That's my burden. Nobody's ever changed that –

JOHN. But if you –

PAUL. We can stop Cutting. But we'll still be the people who used to Cut. You'll still be the people who used to be Cut. Always the same. No fucking point. We soften the blow. Maybe we end the Cut. But still the old circles, the old divides. Young and I thought – change it all. I can make it all better. Nothing's going to be the same. Out with the last lot. And now look at me. Repellent. Can't tell my beautiful wife, my beautiful children –

JOHN. Listen, listen, listen.

PAUL. What does it matter? Send my beautiful children to the prison or the university, still they'll be…

JOHN. Listen to me.

PAUL. They'll always be Cutters, never Cut.

JOHN. I want to show you.

PAUL. The old lot, the new lot. Everything's the same. We've changed nothing.

JOHN. Ssssh. Ssssh. I've got something to show you.

PAUL. Yes?

JOHN. Yes. I've discovered… I want to share… I always knew what the Cut was going to be, okay?

PAUL. Alright.

JOHN. Liberty. Freedom. Nothingness. I knew that. Don't ask me how. But from dot I knew, so I…

PAUL. Yes?

JOHN. Prepared myself. Practiced little moments of emptiness. Not forever like the Cut but moments. And you can do that.

PAUL. I can't.

JOHN. You can. Each of us can. Each and every one of us can free ourselves.

PAUL. Not me.

JOHN. If only you'll…shut your eyes.

PAUL. No.

JOHN. Please.

PAUL. No. I'm sorry. But you understand. After the incident. With the gun. After the incident with the gun I find trust impossible.

JOHN. Of course.

PAUL. Which has made lovemaking with my wife, which has made it – does this embarrass you?

JOHN. No no.

PAUL. Which has made lovemaking with my wife impossible. It's only when you can't…when you can no longer close your eyes during the, the, the…act that you realise… lovemaking with the eyes wide open…impossible.

JOHN. I see.

PAUL. Unnerving for her, embarrassing for me.

JOHN. Of course. I've been searched.

PAUL. But if you strangled me.

JOHN. Beat me away. Beat me to the ground. Beat me to death. I'm weak. You're strong. You can easily beat me.

PAUL. Yes yes I suppose I can.

JOHN. But I'm not going to strangle you.

PAUL. No?

JOHN. No. Now please. The eyes.

(**PAUL** *closes his eyes.*)

(*Long silence.*)

JOHN. And there's total darkness.

PAUL. Well, almost.

JOHN. Please don't speak. That's vital. It's vital that you don't speak.

PAUL. I understand.

JOHN. Ah hah. Total darkness. And you have no body. Your body has dissolved. Dissolved or melted away. Every piece of skin or bone or hair. Every last cell gone away. The cage has vanished. And you are free.

Feel the darkness. Feel the void.

Remember how they used to scare you with that? Remember then how you used to scare yourself with that?

The darkness. Where the monsters live. Where the witches live. Where the paedophiles are. The darkness. Don't go into the darkness. Carry the candle. Leave a light in the window. Take a torch into the woods.

Lies. All of it lies.

The void. It'll eat you up. The chasm that swallows the sailors, swallows the ships, swallows the astronauts. The hole, the pit, the gap. Avoid. Avoid. Avoid. Take a map, make a rope bridge. Steer clear of the void.

Lies lies all of it lies.

They've told you lies and you've kept your eyes open. When all freedom asked of you was to close your eyes.

And now you've closed them. And you've made a start.

But still you're trying to work out where the light switch is. Still the torch is in your hand. Still you're fingering the switch. In case. In case. In case.

Don't. Please. I beg you. Spin around. Spin around until you're dizzy and there's no light switch. Let the torch fall from your hand. Let it roll away into the forest. Let the mud suck it up and rot it away.

And stand in the darkness. And become the darkness.

The truth.

And feel everything go.

There's no history. All that struggling to move forward, to expand, to progress. That's gone away.

And there's no society. All the prisons and the universities have fallen down or been exploded. Or maybe they never were. It doesn't matter.

The truth.

And your wife and your children. Eaten away by cancers or burnt to nothing or maybe never born. Generation after generation never born. Back and back until the first stroke of the first day of the first time. None of it ever was.

The truth.

And so there's nothing.

Don't fight. Don't try and feel your body. Don't reach for the reports. Don't try and call your wife.

Because it's all nothing.

There's only truth. There's only you.

Darkness is light. Void is everything. You are truth.

 *(Long silence.)*

And open your eyes.

And open your eyes.

And open your eyes.

**PAUL.** I don't want to.

**JOHN.** Open them.

**PAUL.** No.

**JOHN.** I've got a gun. In my hand. Pointing at you. I'm squeezing the trigger.

 **(PAUL** *opens his eyes.)*

Sorry. I had to –

**PAUL.** No gun? No gun? Where's the fucking gun? You said there was a –

**JOHN.** Yes because you wouldn't –

**PAUL.** Listen son don't fuck around. If there's a gun then have a fucking gun, okay? Okay? Okay?

**JOHN.** I was just trying.

**PAUL.** Fuck. I wanted to… I didn't want to open my…why did you make…?

**JOHN.** Because it's not healthy.

**PAUL.** Healthy? Healthy? Healthy? Fuck you. Fuck you. Fuck you. Sorry. Sorry. Sorry.

 *(Pause.)*

I'm sorry. I really wanted… I just wanted you to shoot…

JOHN. It was a tactic.

PAUL. Really thought you'd shoot me. That's what I wanted. I wanted to be shot with my eyes shut.

JOHN. I wouldn't do that.

PAUL. But then – cunt that I am – I opened my eyes. Fucked up. Because I'm – what? – a coward. And you – cunt – no gun. We're both cunts. Everyone's cunts. Everything's a cunt. The whole shebang is one big fucking cunting cunty cunt.

JOHN. No no.

PAUL. Because that's what you're…preaching, isn't it? In your…sermon.

JOHN. I don't use words like that.

PAUL. But you are. That's what you're saying. Everything's shit. Everything's fucked up. There's nothing worth crap.

JOHN. No no.

PAUL. We've tried everything and it's all a void. That's what you said.

JOHN. No I didn't. No I didn't.

PAUL. Yes you did. Please don't correct me. I know. I know. What were you doing? Talking. Blah. Blah. Blah. But I. I was listening. With my eyes shut. And I know what I heard.

JOHN. From your perspective.

PAUL. The truth. Everything's finished. Everything's over. We're all done.

JOHN. You're twisting everything –

PAUL. Listen son. I'm old. I'm wise. You gibber. I shift the shit and pick out the gems. Okay? Okay? Okay?

JOHN. Okay.

PAUL. And you're right. And I admire you. I revere you. To say what's been in my head, what I've never been able to…the articulation. Because as you said I was afraid and I have been lied to. For generations.

And there in the dark. In the moment. I saw. I'm worthless.

I'm a piece of shit. I'm a speck of shit on a lump of shit on a piece of shit. I'm nothing.

And I don't want to carry on.

And I do have…

(**PAUL** *produces a gun.*)

Shoot me.

JOHN. No.

PAUL. As an act of kindness.

JOHN. No. I'm not an emotional –

PAUL. Yes yes yes. Go. Off you go.

JOHN. No.

PAUL. It's going to get very bloody in here. I'm going for the head. Blood and brains all over the place. And I don't want you to be a part of that.

JOHN. You mustn't.

PAUL. Here. I'll stamp your report. Show it to the girl on the desk. She'll give you your travel money home. We pay reasonable second class fares. Go back to your village – I take it you have a village and a, and a family.

JOHN. No.

PAUL. Alright. You might want to stand back. Blood in your hair and so on.

JOHN. Don't be so…don't be so…no no no. I'm here. I'm here for the Cut. That's what I'm here for. That's what you're supposed to do. You're supposed to administer the Cut.

PAUL. I'm supposed to…

JOHN. That's your duty. That's your calling. That's why you were chosen.

PAUL. Yes well I'm…

JOHN. And that's why I'm here. That's what I've waited so long for. This is what I've been planning for.

PAUL. I'm sorry. Things change.

JOHN. No no no. The clips, the books, waiting, waiting, planning, planning. Every moment I ever lived for this moment, you can't oh please oh please oh please oh please oh please…

PAUL. There's a tear.

JOHN. Yes.

PAUL. You've got a tear.

JOHN. Yes.

PAUL. That's very emotional…

JOHN. I know. Sorry. Sorry. Where's Gita? Where are the instruments?

PAUL. They're being sterilised.

JOHN. Please. Bring them in.

PAUL. We have to reuse them. Public finances. But also sterilise them. Public health.

JOHN. I understand. Please. Show me the instruments.

PAUL. You're a very selfish young man.

JOHN. Yes.

PAUL. To ride roughshod over my suffering.

JOHN. I know, I know.

PAUL. Have you any idea of the burden for a man – of my class?

JOHN. No.

PAUL. No no you don't. Very well.

(**PAUL** *rings a bell.*)

JOHN. Thank you.

PAUL. This evening I shall eat a meal with my wife. We have drinks first. Then a meal. Then I shall read. Then I'll – We'll sleep in a bed. With my wife. But all the time I'll be suffering. Like nobody can believe. And I'll wake up tomorrow. And I'll say: today I'll shoot myself. That kid who got the Cut was right. I should shoot myself.

JOHN. Are the instruments…?

PAUL. Coming. The kid was right. I should shoot myself. But I won't. Oh, I'll look at the gun. I'll handle it. All day long under the desk I'll be handling the gun. But I won't fire. I won't fire tomorrow or the next day or the next day or the next day or the next day. Or never. I'll be permanently not shooting myself. Can you imagine the horror of that? No you can't. Of course you can't. You. You. You…shit.

(*Enter* **GITA**, *carrying the instruments.*)

Ah, Gita, thank you, thank you. Gita's just joined us. She's still training but she's doing very well. Down there Gita.

(**GITA** *places the instruments down and steps back.*)

JOHN. Can I touch them?

PAUL. Well it's not a regular…

JOHN. Please.

PAUL. Of course. No, no Gita. It's alright. Stay.

(**JOHN** *picks up the instruments.*)

JOHN. These are…twenty-three years old.

PAUL. Public finances. Lack of investment.

JOHN. From a workshop in the north. The northwestern workshop.

PAUL. Very impressive.

JOHN. Look at them. Just look.

PAUL. I'm afraid they're purely functional to me.

JOHN. No no no. Classic craftsmanship. This is an honour. Thank you. Thank you.

PAUL. Shall we get on with it?

JOHN. Yes.

PAUL. Gita.

(**GITA** *comes forward.*)

I envy you. I envy everything about you. If you could give me a word. Just a word so I can shoot myself.

**JOHN**. No.

**PAUL**. You've broken me.

**JOHN**. I didn't mean to.

**PAUL**. That doesn't make it any fucking better. Gita. The lights.

(**GITA** *switches off the lights. Total darkness.*)

**PAUL**. You are here for the Cut. Please prepare yourself for the Cut.

(*Long long pause.*)

**PAUL**. I don't want to…

**JOHN**. You have to.

**PAUL**. Please I can't…

**JOHN**. Now. Do it now.

**PAUL**. Fuck it. Fuck it. Fuck it. The Cut is about to take place.

(*Long long pause.* **JOHN** *gasps as the instruments go in.*)

**JOHN**. Thank you. Thank you. Thank you.

## Scene Two

*(PAUL's flat. PAUL and SUSAN.)*

SUSAN. She's like a child. Quite honestly like a simple little child. I walk in and she's looking at it boiling over. Actually standing there and watching – just...watching as it's boiling over. And I say, "Mina – the soup's boiling over'" and she says "Yes miss" and then she carries on, carries on looking.

PAUL. Mmmmm.

SUSAN. And I suppose I should have been angry. I suppose angry would have been an altogether appropriate response. Would you have been angry?

PAUL. Well...

SUSAN. I think you might have been. I think you might have flown into one of your rages.

PAUL. Well...

SUSAN. Oh yes I can see you now tearing into her. Just tearing straight into her.

PAUL. I don't know.

SUSAN. But somehow I... I... I smiled, maybe – I think I laughed a bit, I indulged...yes, alright, I indulged... and I said "maybe if you took it off the...you see?"

PAUL. Mmmmmmmm...

SUSAN. And she did. She did when I actually told her what to do.

PAUL. Well good.

SUSAN. But of course tomorrow we'll be right back to square one. She'll be watching it boil over all over again. Little goldfish.

PAUL. Yes.

SUSAN. It's a great pressure on me. This watching. All the time watching, guiding. There's a burden.

PAUL. Of course.

SUSAN. Sometimes half an hour with her… I have to lie down. In the dark. For several hours.

PAUL. We could have her reassigned.

SUSAN. I went to the hospital.

PAUL. Shall I look into having her reassigned?

SUSAN. I went to the hospital. But really I was fobbed off. A few tablets. They're useless.

PAUL. Let's get her reassigned.

SUSAN. And can you imagine the fuss?

PAUL. There needn't be a fuss.

SUSAN. You haven't seen the family. You're never here when the… Oh there's a father. And a mother. And a brother. I suspect that she has a child.

PAUL. Really?

SUSAN. I suspect. Just a… And they'll all be round here crying and pleading and looking and…

PAUL. Really? Really? Really?

SUSAN. You don't know. You just don't know. Oh yes. I don't think I can handle the fuss.

PAUL. So we'll keep her?

SUSAN. I don't know. I don't know. I suppose. I suppose we must. I suppose I'll just have to do the best I can.

PAUL. You're a remarkable person.

SUSAN. Thank you.

PAUL. No. I mean it. You're a remarkable person. And I appreciate what you do. For us.

SUSAN. Supper will be late.

PAUL. I just want you to know…you're valued.

SUSAN. After the soup and everything…there'll be a wait for supper.

PAUL. Ah well.

SUSAN. So just try…try not to get angry until the food arrives.

PAUL. I'm not going to…

**SUSAN.** I know you, I know you. Your blood sugar…if the blood sugar's not even that's when you start to get…

**PAUL.** What? What?

**SUSAN.** You get tetchy.

**PAUL.** No. No. No.

**SUSAN.** It's always the same. Yes. Yes. Yes. You're always the same. So just hold on.

**PAUL.** You know me.

**SUSAN.** Oh yes.

**PAUL.** You know me very well.

**SUSAN.** I know you totally.

**PAUL.** Ah.

**SUSAN.** I know you absolutely and totally.

**PAUL.** Yes. Yes. Is that boring?

**SUSAN.** Darling…

**PAUL.** A man with no secrets?

**SUSAN.** Darling.

**PAUL.** Is it dull to have no doors left to open?

**SUSAN.** It's…comfortable. I'd say we're comfortable. Wouldn't you say we're comfortable?

**PAUL.** Yes.

**SUSAN.** Yes. Comfortable's the word.

**PAUL.** But physically…

**SUSAN.** You know there's a big push now. From the universities. I got a letter from Stephen.

**PAUL.** Mmmmm?

**SUSAN.** Today. Stephen wrote from the university. He's looking forward to his fruit cake. Stephen wrote and he said there's a big push now in the universities. The students mainly. But also the lecturers. And there's a big push against the Cut.

**PAUL.** Really?

**SUSAN.** Yes. That's what he said.

**PAUL.** Really?

SUSAN. Yes. There's a real groundswell of...there's a real mood for ending the whole thing.

PAUL. Really?

SUSAN. What do you think?

PAUL. If that's what Stephen –

SUSAN. Yes. But what do you think?

PAUL. I think, I think –

SUSAN. I think they're right. I think they're absolutely...

PAUL. Really? Really?

SUSAN. I think these reforms, these, these, these new criteria... I mean softening the blow I think that's... I think that's...dressing...and I think it's time...

PAUL. What's he doing?

SUSAN. Mmmm?

PAUL. What's Stephen...?

SUSAN. I don't...writing...stuff...they have papers and... discussions and... I don't...

PAUL. So...talking?

SUSAN. Talking and writing. Yes. Yes.

PAUL. Ah. Ah. Ah. Ah. Student stuff.

SUSAN. It's a start.

PAUL. Is it? Is it? Is it?

SUSAN. Shall I hurry her along?

PAUL. What?

SUSAN. Mina. Shall I hurry her along?

PAUL. Why?

SUSAN. You're getting tetchy. It's starting.

PAUL. No.

SUSAN. I can see it. The blood sugar's...dropping. There's a...you're starting to snap.

PAUL. No. No. It's just...politics.

SUSAN. Yes?

PAUL. It makes me uncomfortable.

SUSAN. I'm sorry.

PAUL. No. No. But I've… I've had a day.

SUSAN. Of course.

PAUL. I've had a day and all I wanted was to get back to you and sit with you and eat and read and…

SUSAN. Talk.

PAUL. And talk, yes, of course talk and so of course I find it uncomfortable…

SUSAN. Of course. What did you do?

PAUL. Mmmmm?

SUSAN. What did you do today?

PAUL. Oh. Nothing.

SUSAN. You always say… Really? Really? Nothing?

PAUL. Well nothing of…numbers, figures, reports, dossiers.

SUSAN. Ah.

PAUL. I've got a title. I've got an office. I've got a big office. But really, really I'm just a rubber stamp.

SUSAN. No darling.

PAUL. Yes really.

SUSAN. No darling. I'm sure… I know you're much much much more than a rubber stamp.

PAUL. No.

SUSAN. I try to imagine what you do. I try to picture it. I lie on my bed in the dark in the afternoon. And Mina is breaking something. She's always breaking something in the next room. And I try to block her out. It's better now I've got the pills. And I block her out and I try to picture what you're doing.

PAUL. Really?

SUSAN. Really. I actually try to get a picture in my head of what you're up to.

PAUL. And what do you see?

SUSAN. Ah. Ah. Ah.

PAUL. Come on. What do you see?

SUSAN. Well darling…

PAUL. It's a pretty stupid thing to do, isn't it?

SUSAN. Is it?

PAUL. I should say so. Pretty stupid pointless fucking thing to do. Lying on the bed in the middle of the afternoon. What the fuck are you doing lying on the bed in the afternoon? You shouldn't be lying on the bed in the afternoon. What's wrong with you? There's nothing wrong with you. If there's anything wrong with you we'll find you a better fucking hospital. A better fucking hospital and find some pills that really do the trick.

SUSAN. Hey. Hey. Hey.

PAUL. But there's nothing wrong with you. There's nothing wrong. You think the world's such a bad place? You talk to Stephen and you think that the world is such a bad place then fucking do something about it.

SUSAN. *(going to door)* Mina. Mina.

PAUL. Writing. Discussions. Just fucking do something. For the losers. Take them some clothes. Go through the wardrobe and take them some clothes. Or take them some food. Bake a fucking fruitcake. Bake a hundred fucking fruitcakes and go out to the villages and give out the fruitcake. And help instead of lying on the fucking bed in the afternoon.

SUSAN. Mina. I'm calling you.

PAUL. I'm talking to you.

SUSAN. No you're not.

PAUL. Why is your life so petty? Why is your existence so utterly meaningless?

SUSAN. I'll talk to Mina and we'll get the food on the table.

PAUL. So meaningless that you have to imagine me at a desk in the afternoon.

SUSAN. Hold your horses. The food's on its way.

PAUL. I don't want the fucking food.

SUSAN. Yes you do. Yes you do. Your blood sugar –

PAUL. Fuck's sake.

SUSAN. Has now swung into the danger zone.

PAUL. Blood sugar in the danger zone? Where do you get this, where does this –?

SUSAN. You're always like this. The danger zone spells tetchiness.

PAUL. What is this? Some clip you've seen?

SUSAN. We need to treat this as soon as we possibly can.

PAUL. I'm not your patient. I'm not here for –

SUSAN. Let's feed you, darling. Let's feed you and everything will be alright.

(*Enter* **MINA**.)

Mina. Mina. Where is the food? The food is very late. We've been waiting. And it's not you that suffers. It's never you that suffers. Mister is suffering because of his blood sugar –

PAUL. Agh.

SUSAN. And Miss is suffering because Mister is suffering and Mister is now tetchy. Bread straight away. Supper as soon as you can.

MINA. *Yes Miss.*

(*Exit* **MINA**.)

SUSAN. Like a child. Look at her. Never really understands.

PAUL. Will we fuck tonight?

SUSAN. I don't know.

PAUL. Really? Really? You don't know?

SUSAN. How should I know?

PAUL. Maybe because…

SUSAN. It's not something we can plan for.

PAUL. No.

SUSAN. I would really rather that was spontaneous.

PAUL. Well let's see we haven't…

SUSAN. I'd rather that was something that just happened between us.

PAUL. It's been six months.

SUSAN. Has it?

PAUL. Give or take – yes, six months.

SUSAN. Because, because…

PAUL. So I should say…six months. At least. More like seven or eight…

SUSAN. No.

PAUL. Eight months. I should say the chances of a fuck tonight are pretty slim.

SUSAN. Well maybe yes maybe.

PAUL. I would say definitely.

SUSAN. Alright then.

PAUL. I would say definitely zero.

SUSAN. Alright.

PAUL. Why is that do you think?

SUSAN. Well because…

PAUL. Why is there nothing spontaneous happening between us?

SUSAN. I should say because…because…

PAUL. Why do you sleep in Stephen's old room, wait 'til you think I'm asleep then pad along the corridor to Stephen's room?

SUSAN. Because…

PAUL. Why have I been tossing myself to sleep for eight fucking months?

SUSAN. Because you always kept your eyes closed.

PAUL. Did I?

SUSAN. Yes. Because your eyes were shut. Not just… squeezed tight. From start to finish.

PAUL. Crap. Crap.

SUSAN. True. True. Fucking true and you know it. And you wept.

PAUL. What?

SUSAN. Eyes squeezed tight with great tears down your cheeks.

PAUL. This is…

SUSAN. Your chest holding in the…some grief. Grieving as we fucked.

PAUL. No. No. No.

SUSAN. Please don't… Grieving as we fucked. And eventually…as a woman…you don't…you can't…

PAUL. Why do you have to spout this shit? Why do you let this crap come out of your mouth?

SUSAN. I know. I saw.

PAUL. Have you ever seen me cry? Do I look like a man who cries? Has there ever been a day…? Christ, we've known each other for fucking generations. Under the last lot. Under the new lot. We've been together for so fucking long. And have I ever been a crying man?

SUSAN. Only when we –

PAUL. So please don't give me this…because I really don't need this, this, this, this shit.

SUSAN. How can you just, just –?

PAUL. SHUT UP. SHUT THE FUCK UP.

(*Silence. Enter* **MINA** *with bread on a plate.*)

SUSAN. Thank you Mina. Did you get this from the –? Well you better get back to the… Mina, there's a chip on this plate. Do you know anything about this chip on the side of this plate here? Listen, you'd better get back to the supper.

MINA. Yes Miss.

(*Exit* **MINA**.)

SUSAN. Look at this. A chip on the side of the plate here. This was a new set this week. Pristine. She worked her way through the last lot. Boom. Crash. Clump. Sometimes I laugh at her. And sometimes I just block it all out.

What can you do with a child? Here – it's good bread. I got it myself from the market. Mina never gets exactly what I want. So I've started to do the shopping myself. As of this month. And actually you know it's not such

a hassle. Actually sometimes it can be quite good fun
bargaining. I think I'll carry on. You need to eat.

> (**PAUL** *takes a piece of bread and breaks bits off
> and eats them.*)

SUSAN. It's amazing how quickly the blood sugar level goes
back to normal. Just a bit of bread. One of those little
miracles. Would you like to read Stephen's letter? He
wrote to me. But I'm sure he wouldn't mind – I think
he'd be happy if you read it.

PAUL. I love you.

SUSAN. I put the letter down somewhere.

PAUL. I love you.

SUSAN. I was reading it – I was here…and then I got
distracted by Mina and I went to the…letter in my
hand.

PAUL. I love you.

SUSAN. And then I was on the bed in the dark.

PAUL. I love you.

SUSAN. And then back in…

PAUL. I love you.

SUSAN. So it must be – unless she's moved it of course
which is entirely possible…

PAUL. I love you.

SUSAN. No. No. Here. Here.

PAUL. What?

SUSAN. Stephen's letter. Do you want to read it?

PAUL. Thank you.

> (**PAUL** *takes the letter.*)

He's always liked fruitcake.

SUSAN. Always.

PAUL. Can you remember a time when he didn't like
fruitcake?

SUSAN. No. No. I can't.

PAUL. Maybe that's why he's always been so happy. Blood sugar's up, eh?

SUSAN. Yes, maybe that's it.

PAUL. I think he's wasting his time.

SUSAN. Mmmmm?

PAUL. Writing. Discussing. Never change anything.

SUSAN. Not immediately.

PAUL. And then you...they actually want it, you know?

SUSAN. They?

PAUL. They want to be Cut.

SUSAN. Hardly.

PAUL. Oh yes, you listen to them. On the bus or...they actually want it.

SUSAN. They can't to,

PAUL. You realise the tradition, the...it actually means something. It gives them meaning.

SUSAN. No. No.

PAUL. That's the reality of the situation.

SUSAN. How do you know?

PAUL. I overhear, I observe.

SUSAN. How can you say that?

PAUL. Because I am actually out there, day after day. I actually –

SUSAN. And I'm... I go shopping. I go outside too.

PAUL. Yes?

SUSAN. And I don't overhear...so you actually want this to go on? You don't want anything to change? You want this practice this well frankly barbaric you just want this to go on and on and on?

PAUL. I'm tired.

SUSAN. Are you actually defending –?

PAUL. I'd love to talk to you. I'd love to debate with you. That would be a great pleasure. But actually after a day of work –

SUSAN. As I see it – Stephen says…you've actually got to be for it or against it.

PAUL. Grow up.

SUSAN. That's what Stephen says.

PAUL. Fuck's sake – Stephen is a child. Stephen is a student.

SUSAN. And I think I actually agree with him.

PAUL. But you – you're a grown, you're a mature, you're an old, older woman, person, I think it's a bit late to be seeing the world in –

SUSAN. I think I may join a group.

PAUL. Black and white. Goodies and Baddies. Us and Them. We Cut. They are Cut. Fucking simplistic fucking –

SUSAN. Or I may start yes actually I may start a group.

PAUL. Life isn't simple. Things aren't simple. Don't simplify – let Stephen – fine he's a student – maybe at the university but don't simplify –

SUSAN. You know what I saw this afternoon?

PAUL. That's all I'm saying.

SUSAN. I lay on the bed this afternoon. In the dark. I took three pills. You're only supposed to take two but I felt… I knew those plates were vulnerable and I was feeling… anyway I took three tablets and I lie back on the bed, I lay back in the darkness and I tried to picture you…

PAUL. Listen…

SUSAN. Which I've been doing quite a lot recently. The last – oooo – six months. Lie on the bed in the afternoon and I try to picture what you're doing at your office.

PAUL. Don't.

SUSAN. And often I get no picture at all. Often actually my mind's still here. And I'm anxious for the crockery and the ornaments and the windows with Mina on the loose. No pictures at all or sometimes a picture, very dull. You're filing. Writing down some numbers.

Few seconds of a very dull picture. That's all it's been before.

PAUL. Yes.

SUSAN. But today. But today. A very clear picture. Suddenly. And you're cutting. There's a young man. And there's the instruments. And you're cutting him.

PAUL. Yes.

SUSAN. In your dull little office you were doing the Cut. And I wonder why did that come into my head?

PAUL. Why do you think?

SUSAN. I don't know. It was so clear.

PAUL. Were you awake?

SUSAN. Oh yes. I was looking at the ceiling. Because I noticed a mark. Maybe it was Stephen's letter? Do you think that put the idea into my head.

PAUL. That's possible.

SUSAN. That's the only thing that I can think of. Can you think of anything else?

PAUL. The bread's all finished.

SUSAN. There's more. Mina will bring it.

PAUL. I think I've had enough. I find sometimes… I get bloated.

SUSAN. You never said.

PAUL. Oh yes. More than a couple of slices I find I have a tendency to get bloated.

SUSAN. You never told me that before.

PAUL. It's a tiny, it's a small thing…

SUSAN. Maybe if we tried another…

PAUL. It's only really started. In the last six months or so.

SUSAN. I see. I see. These things are sent to try us, aren't they?

PAUL. I suppose that's right. Yes. These things are sent to try us. I thought of you this afternoon.

SUSAN. Really?

PAUL. Physically. I thought about you physically this afternoon.

SUSAN. We'll try another kind of bread.

PAUL. And I resolved… I'd like us to try again…physically I'd like us to have another go.

SUSAN. Oh.

PAUL. I'd like us to pick up where we left off. Lovemaking.

SUSAN. That's what you did in your office? Thought about us lovemaking?

PAUL. Yes, yes I did.

SUSAN. That was rather naughty.

PAUL. Yes yes it was.

SUSAN. And here was I. Lying in the bed. Seeing you do the Cut.

PAUL. Well.

SUSAN. Well.

(*Enter* **MINA** *with a tray with two main courses and cutlery.*)

Thank you Mina. Better late than…there's a good girl. On the table.

(**MINA** *lays the table.*)

That's it, very good. Do you have a little girl or a little boy, Mina? Which is it? Boy or a girl? I tease her about it all day long. Don't I, Mina? Boy or girl, Mina? Boy or a girl? But she won't tell. You keep your secrets don't you Mina? You keep your cards close to your chest. But you've got a little kiddy tucked away at home. I know you do. I've got an instinct. There are no secrets from me are there? I reckon a boy. We've got two boys. Do you want your boy to have the Cut, Mina? Like his ancestors. Course you don't. Makes you scared. Makes you angry. The Cut. Doesn't it, Mina? Well don't you worry Mina. Because that's all going to end. That's all going to change. My son's working on that. I'm working on that. We're going to get rid of the Cut. We're going to hunt them down and chuck them out. There'll be none of them left. There'll be none of them doing the Cut by the time your boy's a man. You'll see. You'll see. Yes. You've done very well. You've done beautifully. Oh, Mina – tomorrow, remind me when I go shopping – we're going to try a new type of bread. Mister is getting bloated so we're going to change the bread. Thank you. You go home. There's a kid waiting for you. Boy or girl Mina? Boy or girl?

(*Exit* **MINA**. **SUSAN** *sits at the table.*)

Well this looks pretty good. Once she gets the job done you know she actually does it rather well. It's just getting her there that's the challenge. I bet you're hungry. Let's start. Darling. Let's start.

PAUL. I…

SUSAN. I chose all the ingredients myself.

PAUL. I…

SUSAN. Bargained for every last bit of this.

PAUL. I…

SUSAN. Meals have tasted better since I did the shopping.

PAUL. I, I, I, I, I, I, I… (*Cries.*) …I, I, I, I, I, I, I… (*Cries.*)

SUSAN. You always feel better after you've eaten.

PAUL. I, I, I, I, I, I, I… (*Cries/howls.*)

SUSAN. Darling. Darling. Darling.

PAUL. A, A, A, A… (*Cries/howls.*)

SUSAN. You've never been the sort of man who cries. All the time I've known you. The last lot. The new lot. The generations. You've never been the sort that cries. How can I make love to you? How can I make love to a man who cries? Who shuts his eyes and just cries and cries.

PAUL. I'm…sorry.

SUSAN. Well of course you're sorry. We're all sorry. But we still have to eat.

PAUL. I don't want this. I don't want…

SUSAN. Look at you. Look at you. Get up. You disgust me. You disgust me when you're like this.

PAUL. Why can't I shoot myself?

SUSAN. That's a self-indulgence. There are children.

PAUL. Why do we do this day after day after day?

SUSAN. I don't know. Because we have to. There are things in this world we just have to do. There are responsibilities.

PAUL. Don't you ever cry?

SUSAN. No. No. No. Not that I remember. Not even this afternoon. Not even when I thought of you…no.

PAUL. I'm sorry. Sorry. I won't do it again.

SUSAN. You won't…?

PAUL. There'll be no more tears.

SUSAN. Well that's good. Shall we eat?

PAUL. Yes. Let's eat.

*(They sit up at the table.)*

SUSAN. Tomorrow is fruitcake day. Baking for Stephen tomorrow. What will you be doing tomorrow.?

PAUL. Same as always.

SUSAN. So I shall be very busy. No time for a lie-down tomorrow. No time to think about you.

PAUL. That's good.

SUSAN. Yes that's good. Isn't it? That's good.

PAUL. I love you.

SUSAN. And then the next day we can drive to the university.

PAUL. No. Please listen. Please listen to me. I love you. And I want… I wish I could show you all of myself. I wish I could let you into… I wish there was no…

SUSAN. Secrets?

PAUL. Barriers. I wish there were no barriers.

SUSAN. Yes. Maybe that would be better.

PAUL. But I can't.

SUSAN. No?

PAUL. I want to protect you. I want to protect us. The comfort.

SUSAN. And is that working? Is…this…the answer?

PAUL. I don't know. Will you stay in the bed with me – all night?

SUSAN. If that's what you'd like.

PAUL. I'd like that very much.

SUSAN. Alright then. Alright. That's what we'll do.

PAUL. I think if we just lie tighter for a night. If we could lie together in the dark and, and, and hold each other then that could be a start.

SUSAN. Do you have a greasy fork?

PAUL. It's a very small thing but I think it would start to make it better.

SUSAN. Good.

PAUL. There is a working party. I heard there was a working party looking into reform.

SUSAN. Mmmmm?

PAUL. Of the Cut. Within government. There's talk of reform. That's where it will happen. Not with the… students. There's a movement within government.

SUSAN. Well…good.

PAUL. I think the days are numbered.

SUSAN. Well don't tell me. Tell Stephen. He's the one to tell. I'm sure he'll be very interested. Will you talk to him on Saturday?

PAUL. Of course.

SUSAN. Well…good.

Is your fork clean?

PAUL. I think so.

SUSAN. Then please…eat.

(*They eat.*)

PAUL. I'm a good man. At the end of the day I'm a good man.

SUSAN. Of course you are.

### Scene Three

*(A room.* **PAUL** *and* **STEPHEN.***)*

PAUL. You still look the same.

STEPHEN. Yes?

PAUL. To me. When I look at you you still look the same. Six months. Sicking up milk on my shoulder. Three years running through the grass. Eighteen. Off to the university. You always looked exactly the same to me.

STEPHEN. Right.

PAUL. And here you are. I look at you. And you still look… nothing's changed. To me. Nothing's changed.

STEPHEN. Dad.

PAUL. But maybe you…what do you…how does it feel to you…?

STEPHEN. Yeah.

PAUL. Does it feel to you, does it feel to you that you've changed?

STEPHEN. Yes.

PAUL. Ah.

STEPHEN. Yes it does.

PAUL. Ah.

STEPHEN. I feel as though I've changed.

PAUL. Ah.

STEPHEN. I feel as though, I feel…the world has changed. And I have changed.

PAUL. Ah.

STEPHEN. I feel that very strongly.

PAUL. Ah. Ah. Ah. Ah. Youth. You're young.

STEPHEN. Not so –

PAUL. But still young. Still young enough. Still young enough not to see…

STEPHEN. Yes?

PAUL. It all comes round again. You do the same old stuff again and again and again.

STEPHEN. No.

PAUL. Oh yes. There's only so much shit in the pot and it's swilling around and you're stuck in there long enough you'll spot the same old turds flying your way.

STEPHEN. No.

PAUL. That's the way it is. You listen to me. I'm an old cunt. And old cunts…old cunts know this sort of thing.

STEPHEN. There's been a change.

PAUL. Ha.

STEPHEN. There's been a change. Everything's been turned on its head.

PAUL. Black is white. Good is bad.

STEPHEN. We're starting all over again. All of us together are starting together all over again.

PAUL. Very good.

STEPHEN. There's a chance together to start to build –

PAUL. Fantastic. Terrific. I'm proud of you. Good with words. You're good with words. You can out-gibber the best. That's good. You were always like that. I can never quite… I always…suspected words. But you – straight into bed with the little fuckers and start banging away. That's good. Good. Good.

STEPHEN. This really is a better world.

PAUL. You know they turn the light on at five thirty every morning? Every morning that fucking thing goes snap at half past five.

STEPHEN. I'll have a word.

PAUL. Apart from Sundays when – o blessed luxury! – it's six o'clock. We're indulged into six on a Sunday.

STEPHEN. I'll talk to them. See if we can sort something out.

PAUL. I don't want favours.

STEPHEN. I'm listened to.

PAUL. I don't need you pulling any favours for me. Don't you do any fucking favours on my account. I'm my own person. You're your own person. You don't want to be accused of, of, of…favours.

STEPHEN. They're, we're not cruel.

PAUL. They'll be watching out for that. You've always got to watch out for that. A new lot. Favours being pulled.

STEPHEN. So you don't want me to try…?

PAUL. I don't want you to try anything.

STEPHEN. Alright. Alright.

PAUL. What I want, what I want, what I want, what I want is for you to, to leave well alone.

STEPHEN. Alright then.

PAUL. Just…let it be.

STEPHEN. Okay.

PAUL. How's your mother?

STEPHEN. She's fine.

PAUL. Good. Good. Good.

STEPHEN. Mina lost her baby.

PAUL. The light goes off soon.

STEPHEN. Mina had a baby. Inside her. Mina was pregnant. But then she lost the baby. Mother helped with the funeral. She dug.

PAUL. Your mother?

STEPHEN. Yes. She dug the hole.

PAUL. Your mother dug the hole? Your mother dug a hole. Oh. Ha. Ha. Ha. I'm sorry. But that is fucking funny. Don't you think that is fucking funny?

STEPHEN. I…

PAUL. No. I'm sorry. Come on. The thought of your mother, the thought of your mother, the thought of her actually standing there with a spade and the earth and the…that is fucking funny, isn't it?

STEPHEN. Is it?

PAUL. Well of course it is. Of course it is. What's...can't you see the humour in...?

STEPHEN. No.

PAUL. Oh come on. Have you lost all...? Laugh for fuck's sake. Smile. Just let yourself...fuck. Fuck. Fuck.

STEPHEN. Everything's changed. Everything's new. And in the new circumstances.

PAUL. Yes? Yes?

STEPHEN. And in the new circumstance it is quite appropriate, it is fitting, it is right that my mother, that your wife, should dig a hole.

PAUL. Listen to yourself. Listen to yourself.

STEPHEN. Dad.

PAUL. Dig a hole? You sound comical. You sound... ridiculous. You sound fucking ridiculous.

STEPHEN. To you maybe.

PAUL. So get down off your high...stop being so fucking pompous. And laugh.

STEPHEN. That's not appropriate.

PAUL. At yourself. At her. At me. If you like – come on. Rip the piss out of me. Rip the piss out of this whole shitty shebang.

STEPHEN. I don't want to.

PAUL. Christ's sake, fuck's sake...is there no humanity left? Do you none of you have a little fucking speck of humanity?

STEPHEN. Don't you tell me – don't you tell me –

PAUL. Alright.

STEPHEN. About humanity. How can you tell me about humanity when you, you...?

PAUL. Alright alright alright.

STEPHEN. When you...the Cut. It's not me, it's not us...we never...year after year...the instruments...

PAUL. Yes.

STEPHEN. Humanity? Humanity? Humanity?

PAUL. You're right. Did you never think…?

STEPHEN. No.

PAUL. All the years and you never thought for a…?

STEPHEN. No.

PAUL. I was a good dad.

STEPHEN. Yes.

PAUL. I think your mother always knew.

STEPHEN. She says not.

PAUL. Every day a little dance around each other because I suspected that she suspected.

STEPHEN. She told the tribunal –

PAUL. Sometimes it was actually quite fun.

STEPHEN. She told the tribunal that there was never the faintest inkling.

PAUL. Did she?

STEPHEN. Yes.

PAUL. Did she really?

STEPHEN. Yes.

PAUL. Well. Well. Well. Well I suppose she would. Each to their own, I suppose. You've got to save your own bacon when the chips are down, isn't that right?

STEPHEN. I think she's telling the truth.

PAUL. Oh no no no.

STEPHEN. I could see it in her eyes.

PAUL. No, no, no, because I spent the years, I had the years with so don't you…no. Lying.

STEPHEN. No.

PAUL. So – this is the bright new future. This is the new world. Kids who can't tell the difference between a lie and the truth. O son. O son, I would weep but there's no more fucking tears.

STEPHEN. The tribunal cleared Mother.

PAUL. Well, that's good.

STEPHEN. But the house was in your name so…

**PAUL.** Ah…

**STEPHEN.** They're using it as a prison.

**PAUL.** More prisons? A better world with more prisons?

**STEPHEN.** There are certain temporary…

**PAUL.** Yes, of course. Of course. Of course. Would you say I'm evil?

**STEPHEN.** I…

**PAUL.** No. Just look at me now. And would you say I'm evil.

**STEPHEN.** I…

**PAUL.** No. The heart. The gut. The soul. Listen. Listen. Listen to them now. And would you say…?

**STEPHEN.** Yes.

**PAUL.** …that I'm evil?

**STEPHEN.** Yes.

**PAUL.** Ah.

**STEPHEN.** Yes. There are systems of evil. There are acts of evil. There are people of evil. I say that there are all of these things. Yes. There is evil. And you are evil. You are it. You are my father and you are evil. That's what I say. Yes. Yes. Yes.

**PAUL.** I see.

**STEPHEN.** That's not personal…please don't take that the wrong…

**PAUL.** It's alright.

**STEPHEN.** Please. I'm sorry. I'm sorry.

**PAUL.** No. Don't be. I bless you. Come here. Let me hold you.

**STEPHEN.** No.

**PAUL.** Please. Let me hold you so I can bless you for that.

*(STEPHEN moves to PAUL. PAUL holds him.)*

Bless you for that. Bless you for that. Bless you for that.

*(STEPHEN moves away.)*

You're honest. I'll give you that. We were never honest. Me. Your mother. The whole lot of us. We were never honest but you're…

STEPHEN. I try.

PAUL. So maybe it's better, yes? Maybe that's a bit better than before?

STEPHEN. We like to think so.

PAUL. Cold but honest. You are the future, my son.

STEPHEN. And you…

PAUL. And I'm…yeah, well, you're right about me. What you say. I'm…yes I am. Totally. In act and, and, and, and…soul. Totally.

STEPHEN. But if you just…

PAUL. No.

STEPHEN. There is Forgiveness. That's what we…

PAUL. No.

STEPHEN. The Ministry of Forgiveness has hearings. You'll be heard. I can arrange for you to be heard. If you say what you've just said to me, you acknowledge, you can…

PAUL. No.

STEPHEN. There is a way forward.

PAUL. I don't want to…no. I want punishment.

STEPHEN. There are no –

PAUL. I want to be paraded and scourged and feel the blood in my eyes and see the blades before me. I want to know that everyone sees my rottenness and is ready to cut it out.

STEPHEN. What? What?

PAUL. I am the dirt that needs to be destroyed so you can be purified.

STEPHEN. What? Where do you get the…? No. No.

PAUL. That's what I want.

STEPHEN. That's so…old fashioned.

PAUL. Yes. Isn't it? Isn't it? Isn't it?

STEPHEN. That doesn't happen anymore.

**PAUL.** I know. I know. So. I'll sit it out. Lights on at 5:30 six days a week. Sunday indulgence. Sit it out 'til there's a new lot or this lot falls back on some of the old ways.

**STEPHEN.** That isn't going to happen.

**PAUL.** It always happens. Sooner or later. Sooner or later when the forgiveness is done there'll be scourging again and I'll be here. I'll be ready for it. It's what I deserve. I'm evil. It's what I deserve. The light's going to go. Any moment now that light's going to go blink and then there's going to be total blackness. So you had better piss off. Go on. Go on.

**STEPHEN.** Dad.

**PAUL.** You don't want to get stuck in the darkness. You go. There's a better world out there.

**STEPHEN.** Goodbye.

## The End